POE: EASY TO READ

EASY

P O E

TO READ

Easy To Read Series Vol. 2

ARK TUNDRA
PUBLISHING

Poe, Edgar Allan, 1809–1849
Poe: Easy To Read / E. A. Poe
Completely revised and abridged text.

Includes explanatory notes.

1. FICTION / Horror
2. LANGUAGE ARTS & DISCIPLINES / Reading Skills
3. STUDY AIDS / English Proficiency

ISBN: 978-91-88895-02-8

Cover Design and Layout: Ark Tundra

ARK TUNDRA
www.arktundra.com

This book is available at quantity discounts for bulk purchases. For information, please e-mail us at sales@arktundra.com, or call +44 (0) 186 55 22 572

The Black Cat. 9

The Premature Burial. 23

The Facts In The Case
Of M. Valdemar 43

The Oblong Box 57

The System Of Doctor
Tarr And Professor Fether 75

A Note On The Text 105

Explanatory Notes 108

The Black Cat

I don't expect, nor do I ask you to believe the wild, ugly story I am about tell. I would be crazy if I did as I can hardly it believe myself. Yet, I'm not crazy—and I'm most certainly not dreaming. But tomorrow I will die, and today I want to unburden my soul. I want to show the world, directly and without comment, a number of events that once took place in a simple household. The consequences of these events have terrified—have tortured—have destroyed me. Yet I will not try to explain them. To me they have given nothing but horror—while to others they will seem less terrible than weird tales. Perhaps there is someone who can reduce my phantasm to something ordinary—a person more calm, more logical, and far less emotional than I am.

From childhood on I was noted for my tame and timid nature. My tenderness of heart was so obvious as to make me the joke of my friends. I was especially fond of animals, and was given many pets by my parents. I spent most of my time with these animals, and I was never as happy as when I was feeding them and playing with them.

This quirk of character increased as I grew older, and as an adult I derived my main pleasure from it. To those who have been fond of a faithful dog, I hardly need to explain the happiness that it provides. There is something in the selfless love of an animal that goes directly to the heart of those who have tried the worthless friendship of human beings.

I married young, and was happy to find that my wife had a similar interest as I. As she observed my liking for pets, she never missed a chance to buy one that was pleasant. We had birds, gold-fish, a dog, rabbits, a monkey, and—a cat.

This latter animal was remarkably large and beautiful, entirely black, and very smart. In speaking of its intelligence, my wife, who at heart was superstitious, often hinted at the old notion that all black cats are actually witches in disguise. Not that she was really serious about this—I mention this detail for no better reason than that I just now remembered it.

Pluto—this was the cat's name—was my favorite pet. I alone fed him, and he followed me wherever I went in the house. I even had trouble to stop him from following me out in the street.

Our friendship lasted for several years, during which my spirit and character—much thanks to my alcoholism—underwent a change for the worse. I grew more moody, more irritable. I had less regard for the feelings of others. I suffered myself when I cursed at my wife. At length, I even threatened to beat her. My pets, of course, felt the change in my temper. I not only neglected but abused them. For Pluto, however, I still had enough, respect not to mistreat him. I made no qualm of abusing the rabbits, the monkey, or even the dog, whenever they came my way. But my disease grew—for what a disease is alcohol!—and soon even Pluto, who was now growing old—was going to face my bad temper.

As I came home drunk one night, I thought that the cat was avoiding me. Then I grabbed him. Shocked at my violence, he slightly bit my hand. In an instant I was furious. I didn't recognize myself anymore. My own soul seemed to have left my body and an evil spirit had taken its place. I took a pen-knife, opened it, seized the poor cat by the throat, and cut one of its eyes out! I blush, I burn, I shudder, as I think of this horrible thing I did.

When I came to my senses again in the morning—when I had slept off the alcohol—I experienced a feeling half of horror, half of remorse. But it was a weak feeling, at best, and my soul remained untouched.

Then I went back to drinking again, and soon drowned the memory of my crime in wine. In the meantime the cat recovered. The socket of the lost eye looked horrible, but he no longer appeared to be in pain. He went around the house as usual, but fled in terror whenever I was around. I still had so much of my old heart left that I felt sad by the hate toward me coming from a creature that had once loved me. But the feeling soon gave way to anger. And then came the spirit of PERVERSENESS. Of this spirit philosophy knows nothing.

Who has not found himself committing an awful act, for no other reason than because he should not? Are we not always prone to violate that which is Law, merely because we know it to be such? This spirit of perverseness was what finally drove me over the edge. It was this longing of the soul to abuse its own nature—to do wrong for the sake of doing wrong—that urged me to continue, and finally to carry out the injury I had inflicted upon the cat. One morning I slipped a noose around its neck and hung it on a tree—hung it as the tears streamed from my eyes, and with remorse in my heart—hung it because I knew that it had loved me, and because I felt it had given me no reason to do what I did—hung it because I knew that in doing so I was committing a sin. A deadly sin that placed my soul beyond the reach of the mercy of the Most Merciful and Most Terrible God.

The following night, I was awakened by the cry of fire. The curtains of my bed were in flames. The whole house was blazing. Only with difficulty did my wife, a servant, and myself, make our escape from the fire. The destruction was complete. My entire worldly wealth was burned, and I resigned myself to despair.

I have stopped trying to establish an order of events that had caused it all, both the disaster and what I had done. But I am lining up a chain of facts—and don't wish to leave out a single detail. On the day after the fire, I visited the ruins. The walls, with one exception, had fallen in. This exception was found in a thin wall, which stood in the middle of the house, and against which the head of my bed had rested. The plastering here had withstood the fire, because it was just recently made and was still wet.

A dense crowd had gathered around this wall, and many people seemed to be looking at a particular part of it with great amazement. The words "strange", "weird", and similar expressions made me curious. As I approached, I saw the figure of a huge cat as if it was a sculpture carved out of the white surface. The lifelike impression was truly remarkable. There was a rope around the animal's neck.

When I first looked at this thing, I was awe-struck. But soon I came to my senses. The cat, I remembered, had been hung in a garden next to the house.

As the alarm rang because of the fire, this garden had been filled by a crowd right away. Someone in that crowd must have cut the animal from the tree and thrown it into my chamber as the window was open. This had probably been done to wake me up. The falling of other walls had packed the cat into the wet plaster; the lime of which, with the flames, had then turned into the figure that I was looking at.

Although I tried to explain it to myself that way, it failed to convince me. For months I could not rid myself of the thought of the cat. During this period, there came back a feeling that seemed like, but was not, remorse. I went so far as to regret the loss of the animal, and to look around for another pet of the same kind, to replace the cat.

One night as I sat, half drunk, in a den, my attention was suddenly drawn to a black object that was relaxing on one of the rum barrels, which made up the furniture in the place. I had been looking at the top of this barrel for some time, and what now surprised me was the fact that I had not noticed the object sooner.

I approached it and touched it with my hand. It was a large black cat, just as large as Pluto, and it closely resembled him in every way but one. Pluto had never had any white hair; but this cat had a large mark of white, covering nearly the whole breast.

When I touched him, he immediately stood up, purred loudly, rubbed against my hand, and was pleased at the attention. This was the very creature I had been looking for. I offered the landlord to buy it, but he said it wasn't his—he had never seen it before.

I continued to caress it, and when I got ready to go home, the animal followed me. I permitted it to do so, patting it as I carried on. When it reached the house, it made itself at home at once, and became a great favorite with my wife right away.

For my own part, I soon began to dislike it. This was just the opposite of what I had expected. I don't know why I was disgusted at its fondness for me. Gradually, this disgust turned into hatred. I avoided the creature. A sense of shame, and the memory of my former crime, prevented me from abusing it. For some weeks I did not hit, or otherwise violently abuse it; but soon I came to regard it with revulsion, and I walked away in silence whenever it was around, as if fleeing the plague.

What added to my hatred was the discovery, that, just like Pluto, it also had one of its eyes missing. This detail, however, only made it more appealing to my wife. She possessed that kindness of feeling, which had once been my unique trait, and the source of my simplest and purest pleasures.

But as my aversion to this cat grew, its liking for me increased. It followed my footsteps so closely that it is hard to believe. Whenever I sat, it would hunker beneath my chair. If I stood up, it would get between my feet and nearly throw me down. At such times I wanted to destroy it with a blow, but could still stop myself from doing so; partly because of the memory of my former crime, but mostly because of my absolute fear of the beast. This fear was not exactly a fear of physical evil—and yet I don't know how else to put it. Yes, even as I sit in this felon's cell I am ashamed to admit that the terror was caused by something as trivial as it is silly. My wife had often pointed out the character of the mark of white hair on the cat, which was the only difference between the new beast and the one I had destroyed. The reader will remember that this mark, although large, had been originally very vague. With time, however, it had taken on a sharp outline. It now looked like an object that I shudder to name—it was now the image of a gallows.

Now I was wretched beyond the wretchedness of humanity. Soon the creature did not leave me alone for a single moment. Then I started to feel the hot breath of—the thing—upon my face, and its vast weight on my heart!

Under the pressure of these torments, what remained of the good inside of me vanished. Evil thoughts took hold of me—the darkest and most evil of thoughts. The moodiness of my temper turned into a hatred of all things and of all mankind. My wife was now the patient sufferer of my sudden outbursts, to which I blindly gave myself.

One day she followed me into the cellar of the old building, which our poverty had forced us to live in. The cat followed me down the stairs and nearly threw me headfirst. In my rage I lifted an axe and aimed a blow at the animal, which would have proved fatal had it descended as I had wished. But this blow was stopped by my wife. Annoyed, I withdrew my arm from her grasp in a rage and buried the axe in her brain. She was dead on the spot, without a groan.

As I had committed this terrible murder, I set myself to the task of hiding the body. I knew that I could not bring it outside without the neighbors seeing it.

Many possibilities entered my mind. At one time I thought of cutting the corpse into small pieces, and destroying them by fire. At another, I decided to dig a grave for it in the floor of the cellar. Again, I reflected about casting it in the well in the yard—about packing it in a box, like merchandise, to have a gatekeeper take it from the house. Finally I came up with a far better solution. I decided to wall it up in the cellar—as the monks of the Middle Ages walled up their victims.[1]

The cellar was well suited for a purpose such as this. Its walls were loosely made and had recently been coated with a rough plaster, which the humidity had prevented from hardening. Moreover, in one of the walls something was sticking out, caused by a false chimney, and made to resemble the red of the cellar.

Without doubt I could readily take out the bricks at that point, insert the corpse, and wall the whole thing up as before. I was not wrong in this calculation. I easily pulled out the bricks with a crowbar, and carefully put the body in against the wall. Then I re-laid the whole structure as it had originally stood. Having obtained mortar, sand, and hair, I mixed a plaster, which was identical to the old one, and with this I went over the new brickwork. When I was finished, I felt satisfied. The wall did not reveal the slightest trace of having been tampered with.

I looked around me with a sense of victory, and said to myself—"Here at least, then, my labor has not been in vain." My next step was to look for the beast— I had decided to put it to death. Had I seen it at that moment, there would have been no doubt of its fate. But it turned out that the animal had been alarmed at the violence, and avoided me. It is impossible to describe the heavenly sense of relief, which the absence of the creature gave me.

It did not show itself during the night—and so, for one night at least, I slept undisturbed. I slept even with the burden of murder upon my soul!

Two more days passed, and my tormentor still did not come out. Once again I breathed as a free man. The monster had fled the building forever! I should see it no more! My happiness was supreme! The guilt of my dark deed hardly disturbed me at all. A few inquiries from people outside had been made, but had been readily answered. Even a search had been started—but of course nothing was to be found. I looked upon my future happiness as guaranteed. On the fourth day after the murder, policemen unexpectedly came into the house and went on to look around the premises again. But I felt no embarrassment at all.

The officers asked me to go with them in their search. They left no angle or corner unexplored. Soon they went down into the cellar again, for the third or fourth time. My heart beat as calmly as that of one who rests in innocence. I walked the cellar from end to end. I folded my arms, and wandered easily back and forth. The police were quite satisfied and prepared to leave. The joy I felt was too strong to be controlled.

"Gentlemen," I said at last as the party went up the steps, "I am happy to have put your suspicions to rest. I wish you all the best. By the way, gentlemen, this — this is a very well-built house." [In the burning desire to say something , I hardly knew what I said at all.] — "I may say an excellently well-built house. These walls — are you leaving, gentlemen? — these walls are solidly put together;" and here, I knocked heavily on that very part of the brick-work behind which stood the corpse of my wife.

But may God deliver me from the fangs of the devil! No sooner had the sound of my knocks sunk into silence, than I was answered by a voice from inside the tomb! — at first by a muffled cry, like the sobbing of a child, and then swelling into one long scream — a howl — a shriek, half of horror and half of triumph, such as arises only out of hell, from the throats of the damned in their agony in damnation. It would be silly to mention my own thoughts. Fainting, I staggered to the opposite wall. For one moment the policemen on the stairs remained motionless. In the next, a dozen arms were toiling at the wall. It fell. The corpse, already rotten, stood before the eyes of the spectators. Upon its head, with open mouth and a single eye of fire, sat the hideous cat that had seduced me into murder—that had sent me to the hangman.

I had walled up the monster inside the tomb!

The Premature Burial

There are themes that can absorb one's interest, but are too horrible to be turned into fiction. The romantic writer must avoid these if he does not wish to disgust his reader. They are only to be handled with care when the truth sanctifies it. We thrill, for example, at the reports of natural catastrophes and accidents, epidemics and massacres. But in these reports it is the reality, the historical fact, that excites us. If they were invented, we would regard them with revulsion.

But to be buried alive is, without question, the most horrible of these tragedies, which has ever been the fate of a mortal. That it has occurred often can hardly be denied. The boundaries that divide life from death are vague at best. Who can say where the one ends, and where the other begins? We know that there are diseases in which a total cessation of all the signs of life occurs, but in which these cessations are just pauses. They are only temporary breaks in the strange mechanism.

Some time passes, and an unseen principle restarts the whole clockwork again. The silver cord was not loosened forever, nor the golden bowl broken beyond repair. But where, meanwhile, was the soul?

Apart, however, from the conclusion that such cases must give rise to premature burials—we have testimonies to prove that many such burials have in fact taken place.

If necessary, I could refer to a hundred well proven cases. One such remarkable case occurred in a city close to Baltimore. The wife of a well-respected citizen had suddenly fallen ill, and the doctors were baffled at what disease it could be. After a great deal of suffering she died—or was supposed to die. Indeed, no one suspected that she was not really dead. She displayed all the common signs of death. The face took on the sunken outline, the lips had the usual paleness. The eyes were lifeless, and there was no warmth. The pulse stopped. For three days the body was kept unburied, during which it acquired a stony stiffness. Because of what appeared to be the advance of rot, the funeral was completed in a rush.

The lady was buried in her family vault, and for three years it was left unopened. At the end of this term it was opened to receive the coffin;—but a terrible shock awaited the husband as he personally opened the door.

As it swung open, an object dressed in white fell into his arms. It was the skeleton of his wife in her unmade burial garment.

A careful investigation concluded that she had woken up two days after her burial. Her struggles inside the coffin had caused it to fall to the floor, where it broke open and let her escape. A lamp, which had been accidentally left in the tomb, was found empty. There was a large fragment of a coffin on the chamber steps that she had used to strike at the iron door. As she did so, she probably fainted, or possibly died, through sheer terror. As she fell, her shroud became twisted in the iron-work. And there she remained, upright, and rotting.

In the year 1810, a case of living burial happened in France, which serves as an example that truth is often stranger than fiction. The star of the story was Victorine Lafourcade, a young girl from a good family—wealthy and beautiful. Among her many suitors was Julien Bossuet, a poor writer from Paris.

He had come to her attention because of his talents and friendly nature. She seemed to truly love him. But her pride of birth forced her to reject him, and to marry Monsieur Renelle, a banker, instead. After the marriage, however, her husband ill-treated and neglected her.

After a few bad years together, she died,—
or at least her condition resembled death so closely that
everyone was convinced that she was dead.

Filled with despair, the lover travelled from the
city to the remote village with the romantic intention to
dig up the corpse and take its wonderful hair. As he
unearthed the coffin at midnight, opened it, and was busy
taking off the hair, the corpse suddenly opened its eyes.
The lady had in fact been buried alive. Life had not left
her, and the touches of her lover had awakened her.
He carried her quickly to the village. He applied certain
methods of reviving her, and soon she was conscious. She
recognized her savior. There she remained with him until
she gradually recovered her old health.

Her heart was not stubborn, and this last lesson
of love managed to soften it, and she gave it to Bossuet.
She did not return to her husband, and without telling
him of her resurrection, fled with her lover to America.
Twenty years later, the two returned to France. They
hoped that time had changed her appearance to such a
degree, that friends would not be able to recognize her.
They were mistaken, however, because right at the first
meeting, her old husband did in fact recognize her and
claimed her back.

She resisted. A legal tribunal finally decided in her favor, that the strange happenings after so many years rendered the authority of her husband void.

The "Surgeon's Journal" of Leipsic — a periodical of high authority and merit, recorded an equally upsetting event similar to the one just mentioned.

A big, robust military officer had been thrown from a wild horse, and had received a severe contusion. It knocked him out cold. The skull was fractured, but no immediate threat to his life could be detected. A surgery was successful. Gradually, however, he fell into a hopeless state of stupor, and finally it was thought that he had died.

The weather was warm, and he was buried in a rush in one of the public graveyards. The funeral took place on Thursday.

On the following Sunday, the graveyard was full of visitors, and around noon something stirred up a great excitement. It turned out that a peasant, while he had been sitting on the grave of the officer, had felt the earth under him move. At first no one paid attention to the man's statement. But his evident terror, and the way he stuck to his story, had an effect on the crowd.

Quickly, spades were obtained. Within a few minutes the shallow grave was so far dug out that the head of its occupant appeared. He was seemingly dead. But he was sitting nearly upright in his coffin and the lid had been partially lifted.

He was brought to a hospital right away, and said to be still alive. After some hours he came to his senses and recognized his friends, and he stuttered of the horror in his grave.

From what he told, it was clear that he had been conscious when he was buried, before falling into a coma. The grave was loosely filled with a very light soil, therefore some air was still admitted. He had heard the footsteps of the crowd above, and tried to make himself noticed.

It was the noise inside the grounds of the graveyard, he said, which had awakened him from a deep sleep. But as soon as he was awake, he became aware of the terrible horror that he found himself in.

It was recorded that this patient seemed to be well on his way to recovery, but fell victim to the fraud of a medical experiment. A galvanic battery was applied, and he suddenly died in a spasm caused by it.[1]

The mention of that battery brings another case to my memory, where it was capable of bringing a young attorney back to life. He had then been buried for two days. This occurred in 1831, and at the time the story caused a great sensation with the public.

The patient, Edward Stapleton, had died of typhus fever. Right after his death, his friends were asked to sanction an autopsy, but they declined.

As is common in such cases, where an autopsy is refused, the doctors instead dig up the body from the grave and dissect it in private. Thanks to the many body-snatchers around town, it was easy to arrange the transfer of the body. On the third night after the funeral, the corpse was then taken from the grave and put in an opening chamber of a private hospital.

A cut had actually been made to the stomach, when the fresh look of the corpse suggested that they could connect it to the battery. One experiment followed another, and the usual effects resulted—with the exception of two instances, where it resulted in a more life-like spasm. It was late in the night. Daybreak was close. It was thought better to proceed to the dissection soon.

One student present, however, was keen to test a theory of his own first. He insisted on applying the battery to one of the chest muscles. A rough cut was made, and a wire was connected to it, when the patent suddenly arose from the table, walked to the middle of the floor, looked around uneasily for a moment, and then— spoke. What he said was impossible to understand, but words were indeed spoken. Then he fell heavily to the floor.

For a moment everyone was struck with awe—but the urgency of the situation quickly brought them to their senses. It was established that Mr. Stapleton was alive, but not conscious. He was then revived and restored to health—and his friends were never told about what had happened, until a relapse was no longer to be feared. One can imagine their amazement.

The strangest thing about this incident, nevertheless, involves the statement of Mr. S. himself. He declares that at no time was he unconscious—that he was aware of everything that happened to him. This, from the moment he was thought to be dead, right up until when he fainted and fell to the floor of the hospital. "I am alive", were the words he had tried to say at that moment, but which no one could understand.

It is easy to list many stories such as these, but I refrain from doing so. Indeed, we have no need to prove the fact that premature burials do indeed occur.

When we think of how rarely we are able to even detect them, we must admit that maybe they happen much more often than we care to know. There is hardly a graveyard where skeletons are not found in strange positions, which suggest the most horrible suspicions.

The suspicion is horrible, indeed—but more horrible is the doom. It may be well established that no event can inspire so much horror in us as the idea of burial before death. The oppression of the lungs—the stench of the earth—the clinging to death garments—the narrow coffin—the total darkness— the overwhelming silence.

These things, with the thought of air and grass above, with the memory of friends who could save us if they knew—the idea that no one will ever know that we were still alive—these things carry a horror into the still-beating heart. We can dream of nothing even remotely as hideous in hell. And therefore all stories on this topic stir great interest. What I will now tell, comes from my own actual experience.

For many years I had been suffering attacks from a disorder that the doctors agreed was catalepsy, for the lack of a better description.[2] Even though the causes and the diagnosis of this disease are still unknown, its character is well understood.

Sometimes the patient lies in a state of extreme drowsiness, for a shorter period. He is senseless and motionless; but the heartbeat can still be detected, some bodily warmth remains; the cheeks retain slight color; and if one puts a mirror to the lips, one can detect a weak breath.

At other times this state goes on for weeks — or even for months, while medical tests fail to establish a distinction between that state of the sufferer and death. Usually he is saved from being buried alive only by the knowledge of his friends that he suffers from catalepsy. Something that is apparent, above all, in the absence of decay.

The advances of the sickness are, luckily, gradual. The first manifestations cannot be mistaken. The seizures grow more distinctive, and longer than the ones before. Here lies the principal security from accidental burial. But the really unlucky one, whose first seizure should be of an extreme character, would definitely be handed over to the grave alive.

My own case was no different from those mentioned in medical books. Sometimes I fell without cause into a half-unconscious state, without pain, unable to move. Strictly speaking I could not think—only with a dull awareness of life and of those around my bed.

I remained like that until the crisis of the disease was over. At other times I quickly became sick. I grew sick, and dizzy, and fell flat again. For weeks all was black and silent, the universe became empty to me.

My awakening from these latter attacks took much longer than the time of the seizure. Just as the day dawns to the homeless beggar, who roams the streets through the night—just so tiredly and cheerily did my soul come back to me.

Apart from the tendency to fall into this state, my health appeared to be good. I could not perceive that it was affected by the sickness at all—when I awakened from the slumber, I could never gain complete control of my senses right away, and always remained in a confused state for many minutes. The mental faculties and the memory were unresponsive. But in all this there was no physical suffering, only moral distress. My mood grew black, I talked "of worms, of graves, of tombstones."

I was lost in daydreams of death, and the idea of premature burial filled my mind. It haunted me day and night. When night came, I struggled to sleep—because I reflected that I might find myself inside a grave when I woke up. When I finally sank into a slumber, it was only to fall into a world of dreams, above which hovered one gloomy idea.

From the countless images of horror that oppressed me in dreams, I select only one that I will retell. I thought that I was in the middle of a seizure that was longer than usual. Suddenly an icy hand came upon my forehead, and a gibbering voice whispered "Arise!" in my ear.

I was sitting upright in total darkness. I could not see the figure of the one who had awakened me. I could not recall when I had fallen into this trance, nor where it had happened. While I remained still, and tried to collect my thoughts, the cold hand took my wrist and shook it, while the gibbering voice said again:

"Arise! Did I not tell you to arise?"

"And who," I asked, "are you?"

"I have no name where I live," the voice replied, mournfully; "I was a mortal, but now am a fiend."

"I was merciless, but am pitiful. You do feel that I shudder—my teeth chatter when I speak, but it is not because of the chilliness of the night—of the night that has no end. But this ugliness is hard to stand. How can you sleep calmly? I cannot rest for the cry of these great agonies. These sights are more than I can take. Get up! Come with me into the outer night, and let me show you the graves. Is this not a sad spectacle?—Behold!"

I looked. The unseen figure, which still grasped me by the wrist, had thrown open the graves of all mankind. From each a faint light of decay radiated, so that I could see their deepest recesses, and there view the bodies in their sad slumbers with the worm. But the real sleepers were fewer than those who did not slumber at all. There was a feeble struggle, and there was a general unrest. From out of the depths of the pits came a melancholy rustling from the garments of the buried. And those who had reposed themselves, I saw that many had changed their uneasy positions in which they had been buried. And the voice said to me again:

"Is it not a sad sight?"—but, before I could find words to reply, the figure had stopped to grasp my wrist, the lights went out, and the graves were closed with a sudden violence. At the same time cries arose from them, saying again: "Is it not—Oh, God, is it not a sad sight?"

Such phantasies that presented themselves at night spread their influence far into my waking hours. My nerves became upset, and I was in a constant state of horror. I hesitated to leave home. And I only did so in the presence of people who were aware of my condition, so I would not fall into a fit and be buried before my real condition was revealed.

I doubted the loyalty of my dearest friends. I feared that they might conclude that I was beyond help, should I fall into a trance longer than usual.

I even went so far as to fear that they might be glad to consider it as an excuse for getting rid of me altogether. They tried in vain to reassure me with the most sincere promises. I demanded the most sacred pledges, that under no circumstances they would bury me until I had started to rot so much, that it would be impossible to preserve me any farther. And even then my fears would not listen to any reason. I took a number of safety measures.

Among other things, I had the family vault remodeled so that it could be opened from the inside. The slightest pressure on a long pedal would cause the iron door to fly open. There were also arrangements to let air and light inside, and containers for food and water within reach of the coffin.

This coffin was softly padded, and its lid had springs that were applied in such a way, that the feeblest movement of the body would be enough to open it.

In addition to all of this, there was a large bell hanging from the roof of the tomb, whose rope stretched through a hole in the coffin, to be fastened to one of the corpse's hands.

But none of these well-made securities were enough to save me from the fears of being buried alive. There came a time, in which I found myself coming out of total unconsciousness and into feeble existence. Slowly, the gray dawn of the day approached with an uneasiness, a lazy endurance of dull pain.

No care—no hope. Then, after a long while, a ringing in the ears; then, after an even longer lapse, a tingling feeling in the hands and legs. Then an eternal period of pleasant calm, during which the feelings of awakening are turning into thought.

Then a brief descent again into non-existence; then a sudden recovery. Soon the quivering of the eyelid, and an electric shock of terror, which sends the blood from the head to the heart. And now the first effort to think. And now the first attempt to remember. And now a partial success.

And now the memory has regained its dominion so far that I am aware of my state. I feel that I am not awaking from a normal sleep. I recall that I suffer from catalepsy. And now, at last, my spirit is overcome by the one grim Danger—by the one idea.

After this thought, I remained motionless for some minutes. And why? I could not gather enough courage to move. I did not dare to make the effort—and yet there was something in my heart that whispered.

Despair—the kind that no other type of misery calls into being—despair alone made me lift the heavy lids of my eyes. I lifted them. It was dark—all dark. I knew that the seizure was over. I knew that the crisis of my disorder had long since passed. I knew that I had now regained the use of my eyes—and yet it was dark—all dark—the intense lightlessness of the night endured forever.

I tried to scream. My lips and tongue moved together—but no voice came from the lungs, which were oppressed as if by the weight of a mountain. The movement of the jaws showed me that they were bound up as usual with the dead. I felt, too, that I was laying on a hard surface, and there was something similar by my sides. So far, I had not yet tried to move any of my limbs—but now I violently threw up my arms.

They struck a solid wooden surface, which stretched above me from top to toe, six feet in all. I could no longer doubt that I found myself inside a coffin at last. And now, in the middle of all my miseries, the angel Hope came—because I came to think of my safety measures. I turned, and made efforts to force the lid open: it would not move. I felt my wrists for the bell-rope: it was not to be found.

And now the Comforter fled forever, and Despair triumphed; for I could not help but notice that the paddings, which I had carefully prepared, were not there—and then the strange odor of moist earth came to my nostrils. It was impossible to resist the conclusion. I was not inside the vault. I had fallen into a trance while I was away from home—while I was among strangers—when, or how, I could not remember—it was they who had buried me like a dog. Nailed up in a common coffin—pushed deep, deep, and forever into a nameless grave.

As this awful belief forced itself into my soul, I once again struggled to cry out loud. This second time I succeeded. A long, wild, and unbroken shriek echoed through the night.

"Hillo! hillo, there!" said a gruff voice, in reply.

"What the devil's the matter now!" said a second.

"Get out of that!" said a third.

"What do you mean by howling in that kind of style, like a panther?" said a fourth; and then I was grabbed and shaken by a group of very rough-looking individuals. It did not awaken me from my slumber—I was wide awake when I screamed—but it made me remember everything.

This adventure occurred near Richmond, in Virginia. Accompanied by a friend, I had gone miles down the banks of the James River. Night had come, and we were surprised by a storm. A cabin of a small boat by the stream gave us the only available shelter. We made the best of it, and passed the night on board. I slept in one of the only beds in the vessel—it had no bedding of any kind. Its width was eighteen inches. The distance of its bottom from the deck overhead was precisely the same.

I found it very difficult to squeeze myself in. Nevertheless, I slept soundly, and the whole of my vision—for it was no nightmare—came naturally from the condition of my position. The men who shook me were the crew of the ship, and some laborers busy to unload it. The earthly smell came from the load itself. The bandage around the jaws was a silk handkerchief, which I had bound around my head, in place of a nightcap.

The tortures that I suffered, however, were without question equal to those of an actual burial. They were fearfully—they were unthinkably ugly; but out of Evil came Good. My soul acquired tone—acquired temper. I went abroad. I exercised with vigor. I breathed the free air of Heaven. I thought of other things than death. I threw out my medical books. "Buchan" I burned.

I read no "Night Thoughts"—no fustian about churchyards—no boogeyman tales—such as this.[3] In short, I became a new man, and lived a man's life. From that night on, I let go of my dark moods forever, and with them went the cataleptic disorder, of which, perhaps, they had been less the consequence than the cause.

There are moments when the world of our sad humanity may look like hell—but the imagination of man is no Carathis, to freely explore its every aspect.[4] The grim legion of burial terrors cannot be regarded as a fantasy altogether—but, like the demons in whose company Afrasiab made his voyage down the Oxus, they must sleep, or they will devour us—they must be forced to slumber, or we perish.[5]

The Facts In The Case Of M. Valdemar

Of course I will not pretend to think it strange that the case of M. Valdemar has become the stuff of gossip. It would have been stranger had it not—especially under the circumstances. Even though all parties involved wanted to keep the affair from the public, an exaggerated account made its way into society and became the source of many nasty lies. It is now necessary that I provide the facts—as far as I comprehend them myself. They are, in short, these:

For the last three years, my attention had been drawn to the subject of Mesmerism.[1] And, about nine months ago it occurred to me, that in the experiments made so far, there had been a notable thing missing: No person had yet been mesmerized at the moment of death. First, it had to be seen whether there existed in the patient any responsiveness to the magnetic influence. Secondly, whether it was impaired or increased by the condition. Thirdly, how far the advances of death could be stopped by the process.

There were other points to be learned about, but these were the ones that excited my curiosity the most — the last one especially. In looking around for a subject, whom I might test these things on, I came to think of my friend M. Ernest Valdemar, the well-known compiler of the "Bibliotheca Forensica," and author (under the pseudonym of Issachar Marx) of the Polish versions of "Wallenstein" and "Gargantua."[2]

M. Valdemar, who has lived mainly at Harlaem, N.Y., since the year 1839, is (or was) noticeable for the thinness of his person.[3] His lower limbs looked like two walking-canes; and he was noticeable for the whiteness of his sideburns, in contrast to the blackness of his hair — the latter often being mistaken for a wig.

His character was nervous, which made him a good subject for a mesmeric experiment. On a few occasions I had without difficulty put him to sleep, but was disappointed in other results. His will was never completely under my control, and in regard to telepathy, I couldn't accomplish anything reliable with him.[4] I always attributed my failure at these points to his poor health. Some months before we became acquainted, his doctors had told him that he was dying. He always spoke calmly of his coming dissolution as something that was neither to be avoided nor mourned.

When the ideas that I mentioned first occurred to me, it was natural that I should think of M. Valdemar. I knew the philosophy of the man too well to expect any doubts from him; and he had no relatives in America that could interfere. I spoke to him frankly about the subject, and to my surprise his interest seemed excited. I say to my surprise, for, although he had always offered himself to my experiments, he had never before put much belief in what I did.

His disease was the kind, which would permit one to calculate exactly when one would die. Finally, we arranged that he would send for me twenty-four hours before his death as announced by his doctors.

Seven months ago I received, from M. Valdemar himself, the following note:

"My DEAR P---,

You better come now. D---- and F---- agree that I will not survive until midnight tomorrow; and I think they have calculated the time correctly.

VALDEMAR"

I received this note half an hour after it was written, and fifteen minutes later I was in the dying man's chamber.

I had not seen him for ten days, and was shocked by the change that the short time had had on him. His face was pale, the eyes were dull; the thinness was so extreme that the skin had been broken through by the cheek-bones. The pulse was barely noticeable. But he retained both his mental power and a degree of physical strength. He spoke with clarity—took some relaxing medicines without aid—and was busy writing in a pocket-book. He was propped up in the bed by pillows. Doctors D---- and F---- were present.

After pressing Valdemar's hand, I took these gentlemen aside, and they told me a detailed account of the patient's condition. The left lung had been in a hardened state, and was entirely useless for all purposes of breathing.

The right was also partially hardened, while the lower region was a mess.[5] It was the opinion of both doctors that M. Valdemar would die around midnight on the next day (Sunday). It was then seven o'clock on Saturday evening.

On leaving the invalid's bed-side to hold conversation with myself, Doctors D---- and F---- took a final farewell. It had not been their aim to return; but, at my request, they agreed to check in on the patient around ten o'clock the next night.

When they had left, I spoke openly with M. Valdemar on the subject of his upcoming end and the experiment that I had proposed. He still declared himself willing and even anxious to have it done, and urged me to start it at once. A male and a female nurse were there; but I did not feel at ease to start something like this with no more reliable witnesses than these people, in case of an accident. I therefore put it off until about eight o'clock the next night, when a medical student, (Mr. Theodore L--l,) arrived. Originally it had been my plan to wait for the doctors. But at the request of M. Valdemar I was forced to go on, and I felt that there was no time to lose, as he was sinking fast.

Mr. L--l was so kind to agree to my request that he would take notes of all that happened, and it is from his memo that what I now relate is either condensed or copied word-by-word.

I took the patient's hand and asked him to state to Mr. L--l, whether he (M. Valdemar) was willing that I should make the experiment of mesmerizing him in his then condition. He replied feebly, but clearly, "Yes, I wish to be. I fear you have mesmerized,"—adding afterwards, "put it off for too long." While he spoke, I began the passes, which I had already found most effectual in calming him.

He was influenced with the first lateral stroke of my hand across his forehead; but even though I used all my powers, no further effect was induced until some minutes after ten o'clock, when Doctors D-- and F-- called. I explained my intentions to them, and as they didn't object and stated that the patient was already in death agony, I went on without hesitation. I exchanged, however, the lateral passes for downward ones, and directed my stare entirely into the right eye of the sufferer.

By this time his pulse was unnoticeable and his breathing was grasping. This condition was nearly unchanged for a quarter of an hour. At the end of this period, however, a natural although very deep sigh escaped from the chest of the dying man, and the breathing stopped. The patient's limbs took on an icy coldness.

At five minutes before eleven I noticed signs of the mesmeric influence. The glassy roll of the eye was changed for that expression of uneasy inner examination, which is never seen except in cases of sleep-waking.

With a few rapid lateral passes I made the lids quiver as in early sleep, and with a few more I closed them altogether. I was not satisfied with this, but continued the procedure quickly.

I did this until I had completely stiffened the limbs of the sleeper, after placing them in an easy position. The legs were stretched out, the arms were nearly so, and reposed on the bed at a distance from the side. The head was slightly elevated.

When I had done this, it was already midnight. I requested the other gentlemen to examine M. Valdemar's condition. After a few experiments, they confirmed that he was in a perfect state of trance. Both doctors were curious and excited. Dr. D---- decided to remain with the patient all night, while Dr. F---- left with a promise to return at daybreak. Mr. L--l and the nurses stayed.

We left M. Valdemar undisturbed until about three o'clock in the morning, when I approached him and found him in the same condition as when Dr. F-- went away— that is to say, he lay in the same position. The pulse was hard to detect, the breathing was gentle (only noticeable by the use of a mirror held to the lips); the eyes were closed; and the limbs were as rigid and cold as marble. Still, the general look was not that of death.

As I approached M. Valdemar I made a half effort to move his right arm into pursuit of my own, as I passed the latter back and forth above his person.

I had never succeeded in such experiments with this patient before, and I had little thought of succeeding now. But, to my astonishment, his arm very readily followed every direction I assigned it with mine. I determined to try to speak to him.

"M. Valdemar," I said, "are you asleep?" He did not answer, but I noticed a movement around the lips. I repeated the question, again and again. At its third repetition, his whole body was nervous by a shivering; the eyelids opened themselves so far as to display the white line of the eyeball. The lips moved slowly, and from between them a faint whisper said:

"Yes;—asleep now. Do not wake me!—let me die so!"

I felt the limbs and found them as rigid as before. The right arm still obeyed the direction of my hand. I questioned the sleep-waker again:

"Do you still feel pain in the breast, M. Valdemar?"

The answer now was direct, but even fainter than before: "No Pain—I am dying."

I did not think it wise to disturb him just then, and nothing more was said until the arrival of Dr. F--.

After feeling the pulse and putting a mirror to the lips, he asked me to speak to the sleep-waker again. I said:

"M. Valdemar, do you still sleep?"

As before, it took some minutes until a reply was made; and during the time the dying man seemed to be collecting his strength to speak. When I asked the question for the fourth time, he said very faintly:

"Yes; still asleep—dying."

It was now the opinion of the doctors that M. Valdemar should remain undisturbed in his present calm condition. Until death set in I decided, however, to speak to him once more, and repeated my previous question.

While I spoke, there came a change over the face of the sleep-waker. The eyes rolled slowly open, the pupils disappeared upwardly; the skin took on a corpselike hue, looking more like white paper than parchment.

The upper lip pulled itself away from the teeth, which it had before covered completely. The lower jaw fell with a loud jolt and left the mouth widely open, disclosing in full view the black tongue.

I believe that no one who was present was unfamiliar with death-bed horrors; but the look of M. Valdemar in that moment was so hideous that everyone moved away from the bed. I now feel that I have reached a point at which every reader will be alarmed in disbelief. It is my intention, however, to go on.

There was no longer any sign of life in M. Valdemar. As he was declared dead, we delivered him into the hands of the nurses, when his tongue started to move. This continued for around one minute. Then there originated a voice from the motionless jaws—it would be madness to try to describe it. There are, indeed, two or three words, which might be suitable for it. I might say, for example, that the sound was harsh and broken; but it was impossible to describe, for the simple reason that no sound such as that had ever been heard by the ear of humanity. There were two characteristics, however, which can put the sound into words.

For one, the voice seemed to reach our ears from a vast distance, as if from deep within the earth. Secondly, it made the same impression on me as jellylike things feel to the touch. I have spoken both of "sound" and of "voice." I mean to say that the sound was one of distinct separation of words. M. Valdemar spoke in reply to the question I had asked him a few minutes before.

I had asked him, it will be recalled, if he still slept.

He now said: "Yes;—no;—I have been sleeping—and now—now—I am dead."

No one who was there even tried to deny the unspeakable horror, which these few words expressed. Mr. L--l (the student) fainted. The nurses left the chamber, and refused to return. For nearly an hour, the rest of us busied ourselves in silence to revive Mr. L--l. When he came to himself, we investigated M. Valdemar's condition again.

It remained the same, except that the mirror no longer gave evidence of breathing. An attempt to draw blood from the arm failed. I should mention, too, that this limb no longer followed my will. I tried in vain to make it follow the direction of my hand. The only sign of the mesmeric influence was now to be found in the movement of the tongue, whenever I asked M. Valdemar a question. He seemed to be making an effort to respond, but did not have the energy to do so. Questions put to him by any other person than myself did not get an answer at all—although I tried to place each member of the company in a mesmeric relationship with him. I think I have now told all there is to tell about the sleep-waker's state at this time. New nurses were called, and at ten o'clock I left the house in the company of the two doctors and Mr. L--l.

In the afternoon we all came back to see the patient. His condition remained the same. We now had a discussion about the likelihood of waking him up. But we all agreed that there was no good reason to do so. It was obvious that death (or what is usually termed death) had been stopped by the mesmeric process. It seemed clear to us that to awaken M. Valdemar would be to kill him.

From this period until the close of last week—nearly seven months—we continued to make daily visits to M. Valdemar's house, accompanied by medical and other friends. All this time the sleeper-waker remained exactly as I have last described him.

It was on a Friday that we finally decided to awaken him, and it is the (perhaps) unlucky result of this latter experiment, which has given rise to so much gossip.

For the purpose of freeing M. Valdemar from the mesmeric daze, I made use of the usual passes. These, for a time, were unsuccessful. The first sign of revival was a partial descent of the iris of the eyeball. It was observed that this lowering of the pupil was accompanied by the leaking of a yellowish fluid (from under the eyelids) that smelled horrible.

It was now suggested that I should try to influence the patient's arm, as before. I made the attempt and failed. Dr. F-- then asked me to put forth a question. I did so, as follows:

"M. Valdemar, can you explain to us what your feelings or wishes are now?"

The tongue shook, or rather rolled in the mouth (although the jaws and lips remained as rigid as before,) and soon the same terrible voice, which I have already described, broke forth:

"For God's sake!—quick!—quick!—put me to sleep—or, quick!—waken me!—quick!—I say to you that I am dead!"

I was thoroughly frightened, and for an instant did not know what to do. At first I tried to stabilize the patient; but, failing in this, I repeated my steps and struggled to wake him up. Doing this I soon saw that I would be successful—or at least I soon imagined that my success would be complete—all people in the room were waiting to see the patient awaken.

But it is impossible that any human being could have been prepared for what really happened.

As I quickly made the mesmeric passes, in the midst of screams of "dead! dead!" absolutely bursting from the tongue and not from the lips of the sufferer, his whole frame at once shrunk—crumbled—absolutely rotted away under my hands. Upon the bed there remained all but a liquid mass of nasty—of hateful rottenness.

The Oblong Box

Some years ago, I boarded the packet-ship "Independence", from Charleston, S. C, to New York City. We were to sail on the fifteenth of June, and on the fourteenth I went on board to arrange some things in my state-room.

I found that we were going to have many passengers, including an unusually high number of ladies. On the list were several of my friends; and I was happy to see the name of Mr. Cornelius Wyatt, a young artist, for whom I had feelings of warm friendship. We had been fellow students at C-- University, where we hung out a lot. He had the character of genius, and was a mix of misanthropy, sensibility, and enthusiasm. And he had the warmest heart that ever beat in a human chest.

I noticed that his name was carded on three state-rooms. As I referred to the list of passengers again, I found that he had booked for himself, wife, and two sisters—his own. The state-rooms were roomy, and each had two beds, one above the other.

These beds were narrow and too small for more than one person. Still, I could not figure out why there were three state-rooms for four persons. I was in one of those moods, which make a man nosy about small things: and I confess, with shame, that this matter of the spare state-room occupied my mind to a great deal.

It was none of my business, but nonetheless I busied myself to solve the riddle. At last I came to a conclusion, which made me wonder why I had not arrived at it before. "It is a servant, of course," I said; "what a fool I am, not to have thought of that sooner!" Then I returned to the list again—but there was no servant indicated anywhere on there, even though it had been planned to bring one—the words "and servant" had been first written and then crossed out. "Oh, extra baggage, of course," I said to myself—"something he does not wish to put in the hands of others—something to be kept under his own eye—ah, now I know—a painting—and this is what he has been negotiating about with Nicolino, the Italian art dealer." This idea satisfied my curiosity at once.

I knew Wyatt's two sisters well; they were good-natured girls. He had just recently married his wife, and I had not yet met her. He had often talked about her, however. He described her as remarkably beautiful, intelligent, and talented. Therefore, I was looking forward to meeting her.

On the day that I visited the ship (the fourteenth), I was told by the captain that Wyatt and his party were visiting it too. I waited an hour longer on board than planned, hoping to meet the bride, but then an apology came. "Mrs. W. was not feeling well, and declined to come on board until tomorrow, when the boat was leaving the harbor."

The next day, I was going from my hotel to the pier, when I met Captain Hardy and he said that, "because of the circumstances" (a stupid but convenient phrase), "he thought the 'Independence' would not sail for a day or two, and that when all was ready, he would let me know." I thought this to be strange, because the wind was good; but as "the circumstances" were not explained, I returned home and waited.

It took nearly a week until I received the message from the captain. When it finally came, I went on board right away. The ship was crowded with passengers, and everything was in a stir before the sail. Wyatt's party arrived about ten minutes after myself. There were the two sisters, the bride, and the artist—the latter in one of his usual bad moods. I was too used to these, however, to pay them any attention. He did not even introduce me to his wife—instead, his sister Marian was forced to introduce me—a very sweet girl.

Mrs. Wyatt wore a veil before her face; and when she raised it, I must confess that I was surprised. I would have been even more amazed if it had not been for the fact that I knew very well not to trust the exaggerated descriptions of my friend, the artist. When he spoke of beauty, I knew he soared into regions that he idealized in his mind.

The truth was that Mrs. Wyatt was a rather plain-looking woman. If not exactly ugly, she was not very far from it. She was dressed, however, in perfect taste. I had no doubt that she had captured my friend's heart more by intellect than by looks. She said very few words, and went to her state-room with Mr. W.

Now my old curiosity returned. There was no servant—that was sure. Therefore I looked for the extra baggage. A cart arrived at the pier, carrying an oblong pine box. As soon as it was taken on board, we sailed, and in a short time were standing out to sea.

The box was, as I say, oblong. It was about six feet long, by two and a half in breadth. Now, the shape was peculiar; and as soon as I had seen it, I was proud of my ability to guess the right measurements. It will be remembered that I had come to the conclusion that it contained pictures, or at least one of them. I knew that he had negotiated with Nicolino for several weeks.

And now here was a box, which, judging by its size, could contain nothing less than a copy of Da Vinci's "Last Supper" — I knew that Nicolino owned a copy of the same painting, done by Rubini the younger.[1]

Therefore I considered this point settled. I chuckled at the thought of my brilliance. Never before had Wyatt kept an artistic secret from me; but here he smuggled a fine picture to New York, right under my nose, as if he thought that I would not know. I decided to question him about it.

One thing, however, annoyed me quite a bit. The box did not go into the extra state-room. It was placed in Wyatt's own. And there it remained, taking up nearly the entire floor — no doubt to the discomfort of the artist and his wife. Especially as the paint gave off a strong and unusually disgusting smell. On the lid were painted the words — "Mrs. Adelaide Curtis, Albany, New York. Charge of Cornelius Wyatt, Esq. This side up. To be handled with care."

Now, I was aware that Mrs. Adelaide Curtis, of Albany, was the mother of his wife; but then I looked at the whole address as a riddle, intended only for me. I made up my mind, of course, that the box would never get farther than to the studio of my moody friend, in New York.

For the first couple of days we had fine weather. This even though the wind was dead. As such the passengers were in a good mood and very outgoing; except of Wyatt and his sisters, who behaved unfriendly to the rest of the party. I did not think too much about Wyatt's behavior. He was even more gloomy than normal—in fact he was cranky. But I was used to that in him.

But there was no excuse for the bad mood of the sisters. They locked themselves in their staterooms for most of the trip, and absolutely refused to speak with any person on board, even though I asked them to.

Mrs. Wyatt herself was far friendlier. That is to say, she was chatty; and to be chatty is no small thing at sea. She became very close to most of the ladies; and, to my surprise, she did not hesitate to speak with the men either. She amused us all very much. I say "amused"— and barely know how to explain it myself. The truth is, I soon realized that Mrs. W. was far more often laughed at than with. The gentlemen said little about her; but the ladies soon deemed her "a good-hearted thing, rather plain looking, uneducated, and vulgar." The question was, how Wyatt had ended up with a woman such as this. Wealth was the general answer—but I knew it was no answer at all. Wyatt had told me that she neither brought him a dollar nor were there any expected at all.

"He had married," he said, "for love, and for love only; and his bride was far more than worthy of his love." When I thought about my friend's words, I confess that I felt puzzled. Could it be possible that he was losing his mind?

What else could I think? He, who was so refined, intelligent, and picky, and who so much appreciated beauty! It was true that the lady was very fond of him— especially when he was not around—she made a fool of herself by quoting what her "beloved husband, Mr. Wyatt" had said. The word "husband" was always on the tip of her tongue. Meanwhile, everyone on board noticed that he avoided her in the most obvious way. For the most part, he shut himself up alone in his state-room, leaving his wife to amuse herself as she thought best.

My conclusion was that he by a freak of fate or in a fit of passion, had been made to marry a person that was below him. The natural result, disgust, had now followed. I pitied him from the bottom of my heart— but could not forgive him for not telling me about the painting. For this I decided to have my revenge.

One day he came up on deck, and as I took his arm, we walked back and forth together. His bad mood, however, showed no sign of decrease.

He did not say much, and what he said was moody. I tried to tell a joke or two, and he tried to smile. Poor fellow!—as I thought of his wife, I wondered how he managed to even pretend to be happy. I decided to ask him a number of questions about the oblong box. It was just meant to show him that I was not in the dark of what he was up to. I said something about the "peculiar shape of that box-," and I smiled, winked, and touched him gently with my forefinger in the ribs.

The way in which Wyatt reacted to this harmless remark convinced me that he was insane. At first he stared at me as if he found it hard to understand my remark. But as its point slowly dawned on him, his eyes seemed to stick out from their sockets. Then he grew very red—then pale—then he began to laugh, which he kept up and which increased, for ten minutes or more. Soon he fell flat on the deck. When I ran to lift him up, he appeared to be dead.

I called for help, and, with much difficulty, we brought him to himself. As he was revived he spoke without much sense for a while. Soon we put him to bed. The next morning he was quite well again, at least physically. I will say nothing about his state of mind, of course. I avoided him during the rest of the trip, as advised by the captain.

The latter agreed with me in my views of Mr. Wyatt's insanity, but cautioned me not to mention it to anyone on board. My curiosity was soon increased by several incidents that occurred after W.'s fit. Among other things, this: I had been nervous—I drank too much strong tea and did not sleep well at night. In fact, I could not sleep at all for two whole nights. Just as the rooms of all the single men on board, my state-room opened into the main cabin. Wyatt's three rooms were in the after-cabin, which was separated from the main one by a sliding door that was never locked.

As we had much more wind now, the ship heeled to leeward very considerably. And whenever the right hand was to leeward, the sliding door slid open, and nobody took the trouble to get up and close it.

But my bed was in such a position, that whenever my state-room door and the sliding door were open, I could clearly see into Mr. Wyatt's state-rooms. During the two nights that I lay awake, I clearly saw Mrs. Wyatt leave the state-room at eleven o'clock each night. She entered the extra room, where she remained until daybreak, when she went back. That they were virtually separated, was without a doubt. They had separate rooms—there is no better sign of a divorce. This, then, was the explanation for why they had booked an extra state-room.

There was another detail that interested me too. During my two sleepless nights, and right after Mrs. Wyatt's leaving the room, I noticed strange noises coming from her husband. After listening to them for quite some time, I soon thought I knew where they came from.

They were the sounds of him prying open the oblong box with a chisel and mallet—muffled by soft wool or something similar.

I thought that I could tell the exact moment when he took off the lid—I also thought that I could tell when he removed it altogether as he put it on the lower bed. After this there was silence. And I heard nothing more until daybreak—unless I mention a low murmuring sound that was so suppressed that I could barely hear it. I thought it was my imagination playing tricks on me. I think it was ringing in my ears, and not actual sobbing or sighing.

Mr. Wyatt was no doubt just giving himself to one of his hobbies—artistic enthusiasm. He had opened his oblong box in order to look at the treasure inside. But there was no reason in any of this to make him sob, I thought. I really believe that it was just my mind playing games with me, thanks to the captain's green tea.

Just before dawn I could clearly hear Mr. Wyatt replace the lid on the oblong box, and hammer the nails into their old places with the muffled mallet. Having done this, he left his state-room and proceeded to call Mrs. W. from hers.

We had been at sea for seven days, and were now past Cape Hatteras, when there came a blow from the southwest. We were prepared for it, however, as the weather had shown warning signs for some time. Everything was tightened together with ropes, and as the wind became stronger, we lay to, at length, under spanker and foretopsail, both double-reefed.

We rode safely like this for two days—the ship proved herself in excellent shape, hardly admitting any water. After a while, however, the wind had turned into a hurricane. Bringing us so much in the gutter of the water that we shipped several prodigious seas, one immediately after the other.

We lost three men overboard and nearly all of the bulwark on deck. We had barely come to our senses, as the foretopsail turned into shreds. But after getting up a storm-staysail, the ship headed the sea more steadily than before.

The wind held on, with no signs of calming down. On the third day of the blow, the mizzen-mast went by the board. For an hour we tried in vain to get rid of it; and before we had succeeded, the carpenter came and told us that four feet of water was in the hold. To our dilemma, the pumps choked and were nearly useless. All was now in a state of chaos—but we tried to make the ship lighter by throwing her cargo overboard and by cutting away the two remaining masts. But after doing this, we still could not do anything with the pumps, and the water kept leaking in.

At sundown, the wind had lost much of its strength, and as the sea went down, we still had hopes of saving our lives in the boats. At 8:00 P.M., we had the advantage of a full moon, which cheered us up.

Soon we succeeded to get the longboat over the side, and crammed the whole crew and most passengers into it. This party left right away, and after a hard journey finally arrived at Ocracoke Inlet, three days after the wreck.

The captain and fourteen passengers remained on board, determined to save themselves in the jollyboat. Once we had lowered it, the captain and his wife, Mr. Wyatt and party, an officer, wife, four children, and myself, fitted into it.

There was no room for anything except a few instruments, some provisions, and the clothes that we were wearing. Everyone was surprised, when Mr. Wyatt stood up in the stern-sheets and said they needed to go back and fetch his oblong box.

"Sit down, Mr. Wyatt," the captain replied harshly, "you will capsize us if you do not sit still. Our gunwale is almost in the water now."

"The box!" Mr. Wyatt screamed, still standing — "the box, I say! Captain Hardy, you cannot, you will not refuse me. It does not weigh much — it is nothing — mere nothing. By the mother who bore you — for the love of heaven — by your hope of salvation, I beg you to go back for the box!"

For a moment the captain seemed touched by the plea, but he only said: "Mr. Wyatt, you are crazy. I cannot listen to you. Sit down, I say, or you will swamp the boat. Stay — hold him — seize him! — he is about to jump overboard! There — I knew it — he is over!"

As the captain said this, Mr. Wyatt really jumped from the boat, and with great effort got hold of the rope, which hung from the fore-chains of the wreck.

The next moment he was on board, and rushed down into the cabin. In the meantime, we had been swept far away from the ship. We tried to go back, but in the tremendous sea our boat was like a feather in the wind. At a glance we saw that the doom of Mr. Wyatt was sealed.

As we drifted farther and farther away from the wreck, the madman was seen emerging from the companion—where he dragged the heavy, oblong box as best he could. While we looked in amazement, he tied a three-inch rope around the box, and then around himself. The next moment both he and the box were in the sea—disappearing, once and forever.

For a while we remained sadly on our paddles, our eyes fixed on the spot. Soon we pulled away. For an hour the silence was unbroken. Finally, someone made a random remark.

"Captain, did you see how quickly they sank? Was that not strange? I admit that I had hoped for his final rescue, when I saw him tie himself to the box and throw himself into the sea."

"They sank as a matter of course," the captain replied, "and that like a shot. They will soon rise again, however—but not until the salt melts."

"The salt!" I shouted.

"Hush!" said the captain, pointing to the wife and sisters of the deceased. "We will talk about this at another time."

We had made a narrow escape and suffered much, but fortune was on our side. After four days of pain, we landed more dead than alive on a beach. There we remained for a week, and soon secured a trip to New York.

About one month after the loss of the "Independence", I met Captain Hardy in Broadway. Naturally, we talked about the disaster, and about the sad fate of Mr. Wyatt. I then learned the following details.

The artist had booked a trip for himself, wife, and two sisters and a servant. His wife was, indeed, a most lovely and talented woman. On the morning of the day when I first visited the ship, the lady fell ill and died. Mr. Wyatt went insane because of the grief. But for some reason he was not able to call off his journey to New York. It was necessary to bring the corpse to the mother. Doing so openly, however, was obviously not a good idea, because most passengers would have left the ship rather than travel with a dead body.

In this tragedy, Captain Hardy arranged for the corpse to be embalmed, packed in salt in a large box, and brought on board as merchandise.

The lady's death was not to be mentioned at any time. And, because of Mr. Wyatts's booking, it became necessary that someone should pretend to be his wife during the trip. The deceased lady's maid took over the role. In the additional state-room, the false wife slept every night. And during the day she performed the part of her mistress, whom none of the passengers had ever met before.

My own mistake was that I had been too careless, prying, and impulsive. Lately it is quite rare that I sleep soundly at night. There is a face that haunts me, wherever I turn. There is a hysterical laugh, which forever rings in my ears.

The System Of Doctor Tarr And Professor Fether

During the autumn of the year eighteen--, while travelling through the southern provinces of France, my way led me to the vicinity of a mental asylum, about which I had heard much from my medical friends. As I had never visited a place like that, I thought this would be a good opportunity to do so. And so I suggested to my travelling companion that we stop and look around the house.

He balked at the idea—claiming that he was in a hurry at first, then he admitted that he felt a horror at the sight of a lunatic. He asked me, however, not to let this hinder my curiosity.

As he said goodbye, it occurred to me that there might be some difficulty in getting access to the premises, and I mentioned my fears to him. He replied that, in fact, unless I knew the superintendent, Monsieur Maillard, personally, there might be difficulty to enter. The regulations of these private mad-houses were more rigid than the public hospital laws.

He added that he had met Maillard a few years ago, and would accompany me to the door and introduce me to him; although he refused to enter the house himself. I thanked him, and our carriage entered a grass-grown by-path that soon lost itself in a deep forest. We rode about two miles through these dark woods, when finally the Maison de Sante appeared in the distance.[1]

It was a fantastic castle. It was quite rundown, and barely habitable through years of neglect. Its entire look filled me with fear, and at first I considered turning back again. I soon, however, left my weakness behind and went on. As we rode up the gateway, I saw that it was slightly open, and there was a man peering through it. This man came out and greeted my companion by name, and they shook hands like old friends. It was Monsieur Maillard himself.

He was a heavy, good-looking man of the old school, with an air of dignity and authority that made a great impression on me.

As my friend presented me, he mentioned my desire to take a look around the premises. Monsieur Maillard promised to show me around. Then he left and we saw him no more. Then the superintendent showed me into a small salon, which was neat and tidy.

There were books, drawings, flowers, and musical instruments in there. A fire burned in the hearth. At a piano sat a young and very beautiful women singing. As I entered she paused, and welcomed me with graceful courtesy. She spoke in a lower voice, and her manner was quiet. I noticed a certain sadness in her face, which was quite pale. She was dressed in black, and excited a feeling of mingled respect and admiration in me.

In Paris I had heard that this institution used a system that was commonly called "system of soothing"— that it avoided punishing the inmates—in fact, they were rarely locked up at all. The patients were given the freedom to roam around under the watchful eyes of the nurses, and they were dressed just as normal people outside.

With this in mind, I was careful with what I said in front of the young lady. I could not be sure that she was sane. In fact, there was something in her eyes, which led me to believe she was not. I limited my remarks to general topics, and to things that I hoped would not be unpleasant to a lunatic. She replied in a normal way to everything I said; and even her own comments made perfect sense. But my knowledge of mental illness had taught me not to put too much faith into what we deem as sane.

As such I continued the interview with a certain caution. A servant brought in a tray with fruit, wine, and other refreshments. The lady soon left the room. As she left, I looked to my host with an inquiring gaze.

"No," he said, "oh, no—a member of my family— my niece, and a most accomplished woman."

"I am really sorry for the suspicion," I replied, "but of course, you will know how to excuse me. The brilliant way how you handle things here is well known in Paris, and I thought it might just be possible, you know . . . "

"Yes, yes—say no more—I am the one who should thank you for the caution you have showed. We hardly ever find so much consideration in young men. And, more than once, the thoughtlessness of some of our visitors has resulted in problems.

"When we were still using my old system, in which the patients were allowed to freely walk around, they were often stirred up by foolish people who had come to inspect the house. Consequently I was forced to apply a more rigid system, where no one was allowed to enter, who was not absolutely reliable."

"While you were still using your old system!"
I said, repeating his words—"do I understand you, then,
to say that the 'soothing system,' of which I have heard
so much, is no longer being used?"

"We decided," he replied, "to stop it several
weeks ago. Forever."

"Indeed! you surprise me!"

"We deemed it, sir," he said, with a sigh, "necessary
to return to the old ways. The danger of the soothing
system was terrible; and its advantages were overrated.
I believe, sir, that we tried it out long enough. We did
everything that could have been done. I am sorry that you
could not have visited us sooner, then you would have
been able to judge it for yourself. But I believe you are
familiar with the soothing practice—with its details."

"Not all of them. I have only heard second-
or third-hand stories about it."

"I may explain the system, then, in general terms.
We never tried to convince the mentally ill that their
fancies were not real. On the contrary, we not only
indulged but encouraged them; and many of our cures
have been achieved that way.

"There is no argument that so touches the reason of the madman as the absurd conclusion. We have had men, for example, who imagined that they were chicken. The cure was to insist that they in fact were chicken—to accuse the patient of being stupid if he did not accept it as a fact—accordingly, we refused him any other diet for a week than that, which a chicken would normally eat. In this manner, a little corn and gravel performed wonders."

"But was this species of agreement all?"

"Not at all. We believe in simple amusements, such as music, dancing, exercise, card games, certain classes of books, and so on. We treated each individual in the same way as one treats an ordinary physical disease. The word 'insanity' was never used. We made it a point to make each lunatic guard all the others. To instill confidence in the understanding of a madman is to give him body and soul. This way we were able to do away with an expensive staff of keepers."

"And you had no punishments of any kind?"

"None."

"And you never locked your patients up?"

"Very rarely. Now and then, if the suffering of an individual grew into a crisis, or took a sudden turn for the worse, we took him to a secret cell.

"We kept him there until we could let him go to his friends—we have nothing to do with raging maniacs. They are usually sent to the public hospitals."

"And now you have changed all this—and you think it was for the better?"

"Definitely. The system had its drawbacks, and even its dangers. It is now excluded throughout all the Maisons de Sante of France."

"I am very surprised," I said, "at what you tell me. I thought that no other method of treatment existed anywhere in the country."

"You are still young, my friend," my host replied, "but the time will come when you will learn to judge for yourself what is going on in the world without trusting the gossip. Don't believe what you hear, and only half of what you see. Now, about our Maisons de Sante, it is clear that a fool has misinformed you. After dinner, however, I will be happy to take you around the house, and introduce to you a system, which is without doubt the most effectual as yet devised."

"Your own?" I asked—"one of your own inventions?"

"I am proud," he replied, "to admit that it is—at least to some degree."

In this way I spoke with Monsieur Maillard for an hour or two, during which he showed me the gardens and greenhouses of the place.

"I can't let you see my patients," he said, "right now. There is always something shocking in such displays; and I do not want to ruin your appetite for dinner. We will dine. I can give you some cooked beef, with cauliflowers in white sauce—after that a glass of red wine—then your nerves will be strong enough."

At six, dinner was served. My host led me into a large room, where many people had already gathered— twenty-five or thirty in all. They were, by their looks, people of rank—although their clothes, I thought, were too rich. I noticed that at least two-thirds of these guests were ladies. Some of them were by no means concealed in what a Parisian would consider good taste. Many females, for example, who were at least seventy years old, were adorned with an excess of jewelry, and wore their breast and arms bare. I saw, too, that most of the dresses were badly made.

As I looked around, I discovered the interesting girl, whom I had met in the parlor. I was surprised to see her wearing a hoop and farthingale, with high-heeled shoes, and a dirty cap of Brussels lace, far too large for her that it gave her face a ridiculous expression.[2]

The first time I saw her, she was dressed in a deep black dress. There was something strange about the dress of the whole party, which caused me to think of the "soothing system" again. I imagined that Monsieur Maillard tried to deceive me until after dinner, so that my experience would not be too awkward during the meal, at finding myself dining with lunatics. But I remembered that I was told, in Paris, that the people in the south were a bit unusual, with many old-fashioned ideas. Then, as I spoke with several members of the company, my worries were chased away at once.

The dining-room itself, although roomy, had no elegance. For example, the floor was uncarpeted; in France, however, a carpet is often dispensed with. The windows, too, had no curtains; the shutters were fastened with iron bars, applied crosswise, after the fashion of our ordinary shop-shutters. The apartment formed, in itself, a wing of the castle, and thus the windows were on three sides, the door being at the other. There were ten windows in all.

The table was beautifully set out. It was loaded with plates, and more than loaded with delicacies. The servings were absolutely barbaric. There was enough meat to have feasted the Anakim.[3] I had never before seen such a waste of the good things of life.

The arrangement was, however, tasteless; and my eyes, used to dim lights, were offended by the glare of the wax candles everywhere. They were placed on the table, and all around the room, wherever it was possible to find a place. There were several servants there; and, on a large table at the end of the room, seven or eight people with fiddles, fifes, trombones, and a drum were seated. These fellows annoyed me very much with their variety of noises, which were supposed to be music, and which seemed to entertain all the guests, with the exception of myself.

By and large, I could not help but to think that there was something weird about all of it—but then again, the world is made up of all kinds of people. I had travelled much and was not easily impressed. I took my seat very coolly at the right hand of my host, and, as I was quite hungry, dug in.

The chat was spirited and general. The ladies, as usual, talked a great deal. I soon found that most of the company was well educated.

My host was a cheerful entertainer himself. He was keen to speak of his position as superintendent of a Maison de Sante. Indeed, the topic of insanity was, much to my surprise, a favorite topic with all the people present. Many funny stories were told, referring to the urges of the patients.

"We had a fellow here once," said a fat little man, who sat at my right, — "a fellow that thought he was a tea-pot; and by the way, is it not strange how often this idea has entered the brains of the mentally ill? There is no mental asylum in France, which cannot supply a human tea-pot. Our gentleman was a Britannia-ware tea-pot, and was careful to polish himself every morning with buckskin."

"And then," said a tall man, "not long ago, we had a person who was convinced that he was a donkey—which figuratively speaking, was quite true. He was a trouble-some patient. We were busy to keep him under control. For a long time he would eat nothing but thistles. But we soon cured him of this idea by insisting that he should eat nothing else. Then he was always kicking out his heels-so-so-"

"Mr. De Kock! Please behave yourself!" an old lady interrupted, who sat next to the speaker. "Please keep your feet to yourself!

"You have ruined my brocade! Is it necessary to make a point in so practical a style?

"Our friend here can surely understand you without all of this. Really, you are nearly as great a donkey as the poor patient imagined himself. Your acting is very natural indeed."

"I beg your pardon! My dear!" replied Monsieur De Kock, as he was addressed—"a thousand pardons! I had no intention of offending you. Madame Laplace— Monsieur De Kock will do himself the honor of taking wine with you."

Here Monsieur De Kock bowed low, kissed his hand with much ceremony, and took wine with Madame Laplace.

"Allow me, my friend," Monsieur Maillard said, addressing myself, "allow me to send you a bit of this white sauce and beef—you will find it particularly fine."

At this moment three waiters had just come and placed an enormous dish on the table, which contained what I thought was the "monstrum horrendum, informe, ingens, cui lumen ademptum."[4]

As I looked closer, however, I was sure that it was only a small calf roasted whole, and set upon its knees, with an apple in its mouth, as is the English fashion of dressing a hare.

"Thank you, no," I replied; "to say the truth, I am not particularly fond of veal a la St.—what is it?—I do not find that it agrees with me. I will, however, try some of the rabbit."

There were several side-dishes on the table, containing what appeared to be the French rabbit—a very delicious Marceau, which I can recommend.

"Pierre," cried the host, "change this gentleman's plate, and give him a side-piece of this rabbit au-chat."

"This what?" I said.

"This rabbit au-chat."

"Why, thank you—upon second thought, no. I will just help myself to some of the ham."

There is no way to know what one eats, I thought to myself, at the tables of people in this part of the country. I will have none of their rabbit au-chat—and, for the matter of that, none of their cat-au-rabbit either.

"And then," said a person near the foot of the table, continuing the conversation,—"and then, among other oddities, we had a patient, who thought himself to be a Cordova cheese, and went around, with a knife in his hand, asking his friends to try a small slice from the middle of his leg."

"He was a great fool, without doubt," someone threw in, "but not to be compared with a certain individual, whom we all know, with the exception of this strange gentleman. I mean the man thought that he was a bottle of champagne. He always went off with a pop and a fizz, in this fashion."

Here the speaker put his right thumb in his left cheek, withdrew it with a sound similar to the popping of a cork. Then he imitated the fizzing of champagne with his tongue, which lasted for several minutes. I noticed that Monsieur Maillard was not pleased at this behavior, but he said nothing. The chat was soon resumed by a little man in a big wig.

"And then there was an idiot," he said, "who mistook himself for a frog. In fact, he resembled one in no small degree. I can only say that it is a pity that he was not. His croak," here the man imitated the sound of a frog, "was the finest note in the world—B flat."

"And when he put his elbows on the table, and swelled his mouth, and rolled his eyes, and winked—you would have admired the genius of the man." He addressed me.

"I have no doubt of it," I said.

"And then," somebody said, "then there was Little Gaillard, who thought he was a pinch of tobacco snuff, and was upset because he could not take himself between his own finger and thumb."

"And then there was Mister Jules, who went mad with the idea that he was a pumpkin. He haunted the chef to turn him into pie—a thing, which the chef refused to do. For my part, I am by no means sure that a pumpkin pie a la Jules would not have been nice to eat indeed!"

"You surprise me!" I said; and I looked curiously at Monsieur Maillard.

"Ha! ha! ha!" said that gentleman—"he! he! he!—hi! hi! hi!—ho! ho! ho!—hu! hu! hu! hu!—very good indeed! You must not be surprised, my friend; our friend here is a joker—you must not take what he says literally."

"And then," said another one of the party, — "then there was Buffoon Le Grand — another notable in his way. He grew insane through love, and imagined himself to have two heads. One of these he said to be the head of Cicero; the other he imagined to be a mixed one, Demosthenes' from the top of the forehead to the mouth, and Lord Brougham's from the mouth to the chin.[5]

"He could have been wrong; but he would have convinced you nonetheless. For he was a man of great speech. He had an absolute passion for speaking, and could not abstain from it. For example, he used to jump up on the dinner-table like this, and — and — "

Here a friend put a hand on his shoulder and whispered a few words in his ear. Suddenly he sunk back into his chair in silence.

"And then," said the friend who had whispered, "there was Boullard, the spinner. I call him the spinner because he was, in fact, obsessed with the amusing but not altogether irrational fancy, that he had been turned into a spinner. You would have laughed to see him spin. He would turn round upon one heel by the hour, like this — so — "

Here the friend, whom he had just interrupted by a whisper, performed a similar thing for himself.

"But then," cried the old lady, at the top of her voice, "your Mister Boullard was a madman, and a very silly madman at best; for who ever heard of a human spinner? It is absurd. Madame Joy was a more sensible person, as you know. She had a fancy, and gave pleasure to all who had the honor of meeting her. She found, after thinking about it, that she had accidentally been turned into a chicken-cock.

"And she behaved as such. She flapped her wings with great effect—so—so—and, as for her squawk, it was lovely!

"Cock-a-doodle-doo!—cock-a-doodle-doo!—cock-a-doodle-de-doo dooo-do-o-o-o-o-o-o!"

"Madame Joy, I will ask you to behave yourself!" our host interrupted, very angrily. "You can either act properly as a lady should do, or you can leave the table at once—take your pick."

The lady (whom I was surprised to hear being addressed as Madame Joy, after the description of Madame Joy that she had just given) blushed, and seemed ashamed at the criticism. She hung her head down, and didn't say a word. But another and younger lady continued where she had left off. It was my beautiful girl of the little salon.

"Oh, Madame Joy was a fool!" she cried, "but there was so much common sense, after all, in the opinion of Eugenie Salsa. She was a very beautiful and modest young lady, who thought that it was ordinary to dress indecent, and always wished to dress herself by getting outside instead of inside of her clothes. It is very easy to do so, after all. You have only to do it like this—and then—so—so—and then so—so—so—and then so—so—and then—"

"My God! Madame Salsa!" a dozen voices cried at once. "What are you doing?—that is enough!—we now know how it is done!—stop it! stop it!" and several persons already leaped from their seats to stop Madame Salsa. All of a sudden a series of loud screams from somewhere in the castle were heard.

I was very much upset by these yells, but I really felt pity for the rest of the company. I had never seen a set of decent people so frightened in my life. They shrunk in their seats and grew as pale as corpses, and ranted with terror. They listened for another scream. And it came again—louder, nearer—then a third time, very loudly—and a fourth time, weaker than before. As the noise died away, the spirits of the company returned. And everything went back as it was before, with life and storytelling. I asked about the cause of the disturbance.

"Just a trifle," Monsieur Maillard answered. "We are used to these things, and don't care about them. Now and then the lunatics start a howl; one starts the other, as is sometimes the case with a flock of dogs at night. Sometimes it happens, however, that the yells are followed by an effort to break out."

"And how many do you have in charge?"

"At this time we have less than ten, altogether."

"Mostly females, I guess?"

"Oh, no—all of them are men, and big fellows, too, I can tell you."

"I see! I had always thought that the majority of lunatics were women."

"It generally is, but not always. Some time ago, there were about twenty-seven patients here. Of that number, eighteen were women; but, lately, things have changed, as you see."

"Yes—have changed very much, you see," interrupted the gentleman who had broken the 'ins of Madame Laplace.

"Yes—have changed very much, as you see!" the whole company chimed in at once.

"Hold your tongues, all of you!" said my host, in a great rage, at which point the whole company remained dead silent for nearly a minute. One lady obeyed Monsieur Maillard to the letter, and held her long tongue with both hands, until the end of the entertainment.

"And this lady," I said to Monsieur Maillard in a whisper—"this good lady who has just spoken, and who gives us the cock-a-doodle-de-doo—she is harmless, I guess—quite harmless, eh?"

"Harmless!" he shouted, in real surprise, "why—why, what do you mean?"

"Only slightly touched?" I said, touching my head. "I take it for granted that she is not dangerously affected, right?"

"My God! what do you think? This lady, my old friend Madame Joy, is as sane as myself. She has her little quirks, to be sure—but then, you know, all old women—all very old women—are more or less quirky!"

"To be sure," I said,—"to be sure—and then the rest of these ladies and gentlemen—"

"Are my friends and keepers," Monsieur Maillard interrupted, drawing himself up with pride, — "my very good friends and assistants."

"What! all of them?" I asked, — "the women and all?"

"Certainly," he said, — "we could not do at all without the women; they are the best lunatic nurses in the world. They have a way of their own, you know. Their bright eyes have a wonderful effect; — something like the fascination of the snake, you know."

"Certainly," I said, — "Certainly! They behave a little strangely, eh? — they are a little quirky, eh? — don't you think so?"

"Strange! — quirky! — why, do you really think so? We are not very formal, that's true, here in the South — do pretty much as we please — enjoy life, and all that sort of thing, you know — "

"To be sure," I said, — "to be sure."

"And then, perhaps, this wine is a little strong, you know — a little strong — you understand, eh?"

"Certainly," I said,—"Certainly. By the way, Monsieur, the system that you adopted in place of the soothing system, was is it very strict?"

"By no means. Our confinement is necessarily close; but the treatment—the medical treatment, I mean— is rather friendly to the patients."

"And the new system is one of your own inventions?"

"Not entirely. Some parts were invented by Doctor Tarr, of whom you have heard. And again, there are changes, which belong to the right of the famous Fether, whom you have had the honor to meet already."

"I am ashamed to confess," I replied, "that I have never even heard these names before."

"Good heavens!" my host screamed, drawing back his chair abruptly, and throwing his hands over his head. "I hope I did not hear you right! Did you really just say, eh? that you had never heard either of the learned Doctor Tarr, or of the famous Professor Fether?"

"I am forced to admit my ignorance," I replied. "I will seek out their writings as soon as possible, and read them with great care.

"Monsieur Maillard, you have really—I must confess—you have really—made me ashamed of myself!"

And this was a fact.

"Say no more, my good young friend," he said kindly, pressing my hand,—"join me now in a glass of wine."

We drank. The company followed our example without hesitation. They chatted—they joked—they laughed—they went on about a thousand silly things—the fiddles shrieked—the drum row-de-dowed—the trombones shouted—and the whole scene, growing worse and worse, as the wine gained the upper hand, descended into chaos.

In the meantime, Monsieur Maillard and myself, with some bottles of wine, continued our conversation at the top of the voice.

"And, sir," I said, screaming in his ear, "you mentioned something about the danger in the old system of soothing. What was that?"

"Yes," he replied, "there was a great danger indeed. One never knows what madmen are up to.

"In my opinion as well as in that of Doctor Tarr and Professor Fether, it is never safe to allow them to run around freely. A madman may be "soothed", but in the end, he is apt to become rowdy. He is very cunning, too. If he has a goal in mind, he hides his intentions with great skill. And the skill with which he pretends to be sane, presents one of the strangest problems in the study of the mind. When a madman appears sane, it is time to put him in a straitjacket."

"But the danger, my dear sir, of which you were speaking—have you had reason to think that freedom is dangerous in the case of a madman?"

"Here?—why, I may say, yes. For example:—not long ago, an incident occurred in this very house. The 'soothing system,' was then in operation, and the patients were free. They behaved quite well—so much so, that a devilish scheme was brewing from the very fact that they behaved so well. And, sure enough, one fine morning the keepers found themselves pinned down hand and foot, and thrown into the cells, where they were treated as if they were the lunatics, by the lunatics themselves, who had taken over the offices of the keepers."

"You don't say! I never heard of anything so strange in my life!"

"Fact—it all happened thanks to a stupid fellow— a lunatic—who imagined that he had invented a better system of government than any other—of lunatic government, I mean. He wanted to test his invention, and so he convinced the rest of the patients to join him in a conspiracy to overthrow the ruling powers."

"And he really succeeded?"

"No doubt about it. The keepers and the patients soon exchanged places. But exactly, actually—the madmen had been free, but the keepers were locked up in cells, and treated, I am sorry to say, in a very bad way."

"But I guess a counter-revolution was soon launched. This condition could not have existed very long. The country people in the neighborhood—visitors coming to see the establishment—would have called the alarm."

"There you are wrong. The head rebel was too cunning for that. He allowed no visitors at all—with the exception of a very stupid-looking young gentleman whom he had no reason to be afraid of. He let him enter to see the place—to have a little fun with him. As soon as he had misled him enough, he let him leave."

"And for how long, then, did the madmen remain in power?"

"Oh, a very long time, indeed—a month at least—how much longer I can't really say. In the meantime, the lunatics had a great time—that you better believe. They took off their own shabby clothes, and dressed themselves with the family wardrobe and jewels. The cellars of the castle were well stocked with wine; and these madmen are just the devils that know how to drink it. They lived well, I can tell you."

"And the treatment—what was the particular type of treatment, which the leader of the rebels put into action?"

"A madman is not necessarily a fool, as I have already observed. It is my honest opinion that his treatment was a much better treatment than that which preceded it. It was a major system indeed—simple—neat—no trouble at all—in fact it was lovely as it was."

Here my host's remarks were cut short by another series of yells, similar to the ones that had taken us aback before. This time, however, they seemed to come from people who were rapidly coming closer.

"Good heavens!" I cried out—"the lunatics have broken loose!"

"I am afraid so," Monsieur Maillard replied, now becoming very pale. Barely had he finished the sentence, before loud shouts were heard beneath the windows. And right away it became evident that persons outside were trying to get into the room. The door was beaten with what appeared to be a sledge-hammer, and the shutters were pulled with violence.

The most terrible confusion followed. Monsieur Maillard, to my surprise threw himself under the side-board. I had expected more dedication from him. The members of the orchestra, who had been too drunk to do duty, now sprang to their feet and to their instruments. Climbing up on their table, they broke out into a "Yankee Doodle" that was out of tune. But at least they played it with an energy that was superhuman during the entire chaos.

Meanwhile, the gentleman, who had been restrained from leaping there before, leaped on the dining-table. As soon as he settled himself, he held a speech, which was a very important one, if only it could have been heard.

At the same moment, the man who thought himself a spinner, started to spin around the room with the arms stretched out at right angles with his body. He had all the air of a spinner, in fact, and knocked everybody down that happened to get in his way.

And now, with a popping and fizzing of champagne, I discovered that it came from the person who performed the bottle of that delicate drink during dinner. And then, the frog-man croaked away as if his life depended on every note that he uttered. And, in the midst of all this, the whinnying of a donkey arose. As for my old friend, Madame Joy, I really could have wept for the poor lady, she appeared so puzzled.

All she did, was to stand up in the corner, and sing out at the top of her voice, "Cock-a-doodle-de-ooooooh!"

And now came the highpoint—the catastrophe. As no resistance, beyond whooping and yelling, was offered to the people coming from outside, the ten windows were quickly broken in. But I will never forget the horror with which I gazed, when there rushed in an army of what I thought were Chimpanzees, Ourang-Outangs, or big black baboons. I received a bad beating—after which I rolled under a sofa and lay still.

After lying there for fifteen minutes, I came to a conclusion of this tragedy. Monsieur Maillard, it appeared, had been relating his own story, as he told me about the lunatic who had excited his fellows to rebellion. He had, indeed, been the superintendent of the establishment before, but grew crazy himself, and so became a patient.

This fact was unknown to the travelling companion who introduced me. The keepers, having been overpowered, were first well tarred, then carefully feathered, and then locked up in underground cells. They had been imprisoned like that for more than a month, during which period Monsieur Maillard had allowed them not only the tar and feathers (which made up his "system"), but some bread and water. The latter was pumped on them every day. Soon one of them escaped through a sewer and freed the rest.

The "soothing system" has now been resumed at the castle. I cannot help but to agree with Monsieur Maillard that his own "treatment" was a very big thing. Just as he observed, it was "simple—neat—and gave no trouble at all—not the least."

I only have to add that even though I have searched every library in Europe for the works of Doctor Tarr and Professor Fether, I have failed to locate an edition.

A Note On The Text

The stories in this edition are based on the original publications, and have been revised to accommodate a modern readership. Care has been taken to deliver them in a way that is both easy to read and a joy to behold, without losing their distinct character.

Just as a Medieval painter lets us see a picture without us taking notice of its brushstrokes, it is our aim to let you read a story without being deterred by its style.

Good writing derives its quality not from form, but from substance. It can be reworded, translated, and abridged, and still be the same; just as the foundation of literature, mythology, has been able to pass through millennia of variations, and still retain its essential core. Or, to mention a more recent example, the fairy-tales transcribed by the Brothers Grimm, whose timeless quality stand in direct relation to the crystal clear diction. Since times immemorial has Cinderella's lost shoe felt more feet than a sidewalk, and still finds the right foot in the end.

While the flowery language of a bygone era holds a historical lure, it at the same time acts as an anchor, whose ship is submerged in the rising tide of time.

The way it was written chains it to its own era, locked in a cell, where its overwrought words and embellished clauses collect cobwebs and dust.

The actual meaning often falls victim to the manner. Style has been more a burden than an asset the past 400 years, and has marred literature to such an extent that many classics are almost impossible to read.

The over-decoration of sentences with empty adjectives, adverbs and nouns often only leaves the outlines of its creations discernible in a black sea of words that have long since gone out of fashion. One can tell the monster from the ghoul, but not the meaning from the word.

Many of the creations, such as Lovecraft's Cthulhu Mythos or Shelley's Frankenstein's Monster, have long since surpassed their literary origin and moved into the realm of modern folklore.

More people know of Lovecraft's creatures than have read his stories, just as Frankenstein's Monster was made popular not by the written word, but by the motion picture. It is time to change his circumstance and let the words speak with a new clarity.

Let us view the painting, as we leave the brushstrokes to the artist, and rejoice at classic storytelling finally unobscured by style.

Explanatory Notes

The Black Cat

Published in August 1843 in The Saturday Evening Post.

1.   Immurement. It has been rumored that in the Middle Ages the Catholic Church immured monks and nuns found guilty of breaking their vows of chastity.

The Premature Burial

Published in 1944 in The Philadelphia Dollar Newspaper.

1.   Battery consisting of a number of voltaic cells arranged in series or parallel.
2.   A chronic illness in which the body stiffens and becomes immobile as if it was dead.
3.   "Night Thoughts" is a book written by Edward Young (1683–1765), English poet.
4.   Carathis is the mother of Vathek in the novel „Vathek," written by William Beckford (1760–1844), English novelist.
5.   Afrasiab was the king of Turan and an enemy of Iran. Oxus was the antique name applied to the river Amu Darya in central Asia.

The Facts In The Case Of M. Valdemar

Published in December 1845 in The American Review and Broadway Journal.

1.   Named after its originator, Franz Friedrich Anton Mesmer (1734–1815), German physician. Mesmerism, or Animal Magnetism, is a hypnotic induction, believed to involve invisible fluids and natural forces in the body. It has since been debunked as a fraud.

2.   "Bibliotheca Forensica" refers to a fictional book, which could be a collection of legal works or similar. "Wallenstein" is a trilogy of plays written by the German poet and playwright Friedrich Schiller (1759–1805), which describes the decline of the famous general Albrecht von Wallenstein. "Gargantua" is a pentalogy written by the French writer and scholar François Rabelais (1483 or 1494–1553), which tells the story of the two giants Gargantua and his son Pantagruel.

3.   A neighborhood in the northern section of the New York City borough of Manhattan.

4.   Also known as thought transmission; there is no convincing evidence that it exists.

5.   The symptoms described are indicative of Tuberculosis.

The Oblong Box

Published in September 1844 in Godey's Magazine
and Lady's Book.

1.　　May either refer to one of several Italian painters
　　　named Rubini, active during the late Renaissance;
　　　or to one of the sons of Pieter Pauwel Rubens
　　　(1577–1640), a Dutch painter. Rubens himself
　　　sketched copies of many Italian paintings during
　　　his time in Italy.

The System of Doctor Tarr
and Professor Fether

Published in 1845 in Graham's Magazine.

1.　　Literally "health house".
2.　　A costume worn by women in the 16th and
　　　17th century.
3.　　Anakim were a race of giants in the Hebrew Bible.
4.　　A quote by Publius Vergilius Maro, commonly
　　　called Vergil (70 BC–19 BC), Roman poet. It refers
　　　to "a fearful monster, shapeless, vast, whose only
　　　eye had been put out."
5.　　Marcus Tullius Cicero (106 BC–43 BC), Roman
　　　statesman, orator, philosopher. Demosthenes
　　　(384 BC–322 BC), Greek statesman and orator.
　　　Henry Peter Brougham (1778–1868), British
　　　statesman, later Lord Chancellor of Great Britain.

A CATALOG OF SELECTED
ARK TUNDRA
BOOKS

H. P. Lovecraft

Lovecraft: Easy To Read

ISBN: 978-91-88895-00-4
104pp, 5 x 8.

Contains *Dagon, The Horror At Red Hook*, and other classic tales, completely revised and abridged.
An outstanding addition to your collection!

Easy To Read Series Vol. 1

Ambrose Bierce

Bierce: Easy To Read

ISBN: 978-91-88895-04-2
118pp, 5 x 8.

Contains *The Damned Thing*, and many other stories—completely revised and abridged.

Never before has the pen of Bitter Bierce been so kind on the eyes.

Easy To Read Series Vol. 3

Visit our publishing site for information
on new exciting titles!

imprint.arktundra.com